The Rainbow Magic Collection

Volume 1: Books #1-4

Ruby the Red Fairy
Amber the Orange Fairy
Sunny the Yellow Fairy
Fern the Green Fairy

by Daisy Meadows
illustrated by Georgie Ripper

SCHOLASTIC INC.

New York Toronto London Auckland Sydney
Mexico City New Delhi Hong Kong Buenos Aires

ISBN-13: 978-0-545-02275-0
ISBN-10: 0-545-02275-4

Rainbow Magic #1: *Ruby the Red Fairy*, ISBN 0-439-73861-X, copyright © 2003 by Working Partners Limited. Illustrations copyright © 2003 by Georgie Ripper.

Rainbow Magic #2: *Amber the Orange Fairy*, ISBN 0-439-74465-2, copyright © 2003 by Working Partners Limited. Illustrations copyright © 2003 by Georgie Ripper.

Rainbow Magic #3: *Sunny the Yellow Fairy*, previously published as *Saffron the Yellow Fairy*, ISBN 0-439-74466-0, copyright © 2003 by Working Partners Limited. Illustrations copyright © 2003 by Georgie Ripper.

Rainbow Magic #4. *Fern the Green Fairy*, ISBN 0-439-74467-9, copyright © 2003 by Working Partners Limited. Illustrations copyright © 2003 by Georgie Ripper.

All rights reserved. Published by Scholastic Inc., 557 Broadway, New York, NY 10012, by arrangement with Working Partners Limited.

12 11 10 9 8 7 6 5 4 3 2 1   7 8 9 10 11 12/0

Printed in the U.S.A.   40

First Scholastic printing, April 2007

Contents

The Fairyland Palace

Maze

Forest

Orchard

Black Pot

Meadow

Tower

Beach

Tide pools

Rainspell Island

Jack Frost's
Ice Castle

Tom Goodfellow's
House

Merry-go-round

Willow
Tree

Mrs. Merry's
Cottage

Stream

Field

Town

...naid
...age

Harbor

...olphin Cottage

Cold winds blow and thick ice forms,
I conjure up this fairy storm.
To seven corners of the human world
the Rainbow Fairies will be hurled!

I curse every part of Fairyland,
with a frosty wave of my icy hand.
For now and always, from this day,
Fairyland will be cold and gray!

Ruby
the Red
Fairy

Dedicated to Joanna Pilkington,
who found fairies in her
beautiful garden

Special thanks to
Narinder Dhami

The End of the Rainbow

"Look, Dad!" said Rachel Walker. She pointed across the blue-green sea at the rocky island ahead of them. The ferry was sailing toward it, dipping up and down on the rolling waves. "Is that Rainspell Island?" she asked.

Her dad nodded. "Yes, it is," he said, smiling. "Our vacation is about to begin!"

The waves slapped against the side
of the ferry as it bobbed up and down
on the water. Rachel felt her heart
thump with excitement. She could see
white cliffs and emerald-green fields on
the island. Even golden sandy beaches,
with tide pools here and there.

Suddenly, a few fat raindrops
plopped down onto Rachel's head.
"Oh!" she gasped, surprised. The sun
was still shining.

Rachel's mom grabbed her hand.
"Let's get under cover," she said,
leading Rachel inside.

"Isn't that strange?" Rachel said.
"Sunshine *and* rain!"

"Let's hope the rain stops before we
get off the ferry," said Mr. Walker.
"Now, where did I put that map of
the island?"

Rachel looked out of the
window. Her eyes
opened wide.

A girl was standing
alone on the deck.
Her dark hair was
wet with raindrops,
but she didn't seem
to care. She just
stared up at the sky.

Rachel looked over at her mom and
dad. They were busy studying the map.
So Rachel slipped back outside to see
what was so interesting.

And there it was.

In the blue sky, high above them,
was the most amazing rainbow that
Rachel had ever seen. One end of the
rainbow stretched far out to sea. The
other seemed to fall somewhere on
Rainspell Island. All of the colors
were bright and clear.

Red
Orange
Yellow
Green
Blue
Indigo
Violet

7

"Isn't it perfect?" the dark-haired girl whispered to Rachel.

"Yes, it is," Rachel agreed. "Are you going to Rainspell on vacation?"

The girl nodded. "We're staying for a week," she said. "I'm Kirsty Tate."

Rachel smiled as the rain began to stop. "I'm Rachel Walker. We're staying at Mermaid Cottage," she added.

"Oh! We're at Dolphin Cottage," said Kirsty. "Do you think we might be close to each other?"

"I hope so," Rachel replied. She had a feeling she was going to like Kirsty.

Kirsty leaned over the rail and looked down into the shimmering water. "The ocean looks really deep here, doesn't it?" she said. "There might even be mermaids down there, watching us right now!"

Rachel stared at the waves. She saw something that made her heart skip a beat. "Look!" she said. "Is that a mermaid's hair?" Then she laughed when she saw that it was just seaweed.

"It could be a mermaid's necklace," said Kirsty, smiling. "Maybe she lost it when she was trying to escape from a wild sea monster."

The ferry was now sailing into Rainspell's tiny harbor. Seagulls flew around them, and fishing boats bobbed on the water.

"Look at that big white cliff over there," Kirsty said. She pointed it out to Rachel. "It looks a bit like a giant's face, doesn't it?" Rachel looked, and nodded. Kirsty seemed to see magic *everywhere*.

"There you are, Rachel!" called Mrs. Walker. Rachel turned around and saw her mom and dad coming out onto the deck. "We'll be getting off the ferry in a few minutes," Mrs. Walker added.

"Mom, Dad, this is Kirsty," Rachel said. "She's staying at Dolphin Cottage."

"That's right next door to ours," said Mr. Walker. "I remember seeing it on the map."

Rachel and Kirsty looked at each other and smiled.

"I'd better go and find *my* mom and dad," said Kirsty. She looked around. "Oh, there they are."

Kirsty's mom and dad came over
to say hello to the Walkers. Then the
ferry docked, and everyone began to
leave the boat.

"Our cottages are on the other side
of the harbor," said Rachel's dad,
looking at the map. "It's not too far."

Mermaid Cottage and Dolphin
Cottage were right next to the beach.
Rachel loved her bedroom, which was
high up in the attic. From the
window, she could see the waves
rolling onto the sand.

A shout from outside made Rachel look down. It was Kirsty. She was standing under the window, waving.

"Let's go and explore the beach!" Kirsty called.

Rachel dashed outside to join her.

Piles of seaweed lay on the sand, and there were tiny pink-and-white shells sprinkled everywhere.

"I love it here already!" Rachel shouted happily above the noise of the seagulls.

"Me, too," Kirsty said. She pointed up at the sky. "Look, the rainbow's still there."

Rachel looked up. The rainbow glowed brightly among the fluffy white clouds.

"Have you heard the story about the
pot of gold at the end of the rainbow?"
Kirsty asked.

Rachel nodded. "Yes, but that's just in
fairy tales," she said.

Kirsty grinned. "Maybe. But let's go
and find out for ourselves!"

"OK," Rachel agreed. "And maybe we
can explore the island at the same time."

They rushed back to tell their parents
where they were going. Then Kirsty
and Rachel set off along a road behind
the cottages. It led them away from the
beach, across green fields, and toward
a small stretch of woods.

Rachel kept looking up at the rainbow. She was worried that it would start to fade now that the rain had stopped. But the colors stayed clear and bright.

"It looks like the end of the rainbow is over there," Kirsty said. "Come on!" And she hurried toward the trees.

The woods were cool and shady after being in the heat of the sun. Rachel and Kirsty followed a winding path until they came to a clearing. Then both girls stopped and stared.

The rainbow shone down onto the grass through a gap in the trees. Its colors sparkled and twinkled brightly.

And there, at the rainbow's end, lay an old, black pot.

A Tiny Surprise

"Look!" Kirsty whispered. "There really *is* a pot of gold!"

"It could just be a cooking pot," Rachel said doubtfully. "Some campers might have left it behind."

But Kirsty shook her head. "I don't think so," she said. "It looks really old."

Rachel stared at the pot. It was sitting on the grass, upside down.

"Let's have a closer look," said Kirsty. She ran to the pot and tried to turn it over. "Oh, it's heavy!" she gasped. She tried again, but the pot didn't move.

Rachel rushed to help her. They both pushed and pushed at the pot. This time it moved, but just a little.

"Let's try again." Kirsty said. "Are you ready, Rachel?"

Tap! Tap! Tap!

Rachel and Kirsty stared at each other.

"What was that?" Rachel gasped.

"I don't know," whispered Kirsty.

Tap! Tap!

"There it is again," Kirsty said. She looked down at the pot lying on the grass. "You know what? I think it's coming from inside this pot!"

Rachel's eyes opened wide. "Are you sure?" She bent down and put her ear to the pot. *Tap! Tap!* Then, to her amazement, Rachel heard a tiny voice.

"Help!" it called. "Help me!"

Rachel grabbed Kirsty's arm. "Did you hear that?" she asked.

Kirsty nodded. "Quick!" she said. "We have to turn the pot over, somehow!"

Rachel and Kirsty pushed at the pot as hard as they could. It began to rock from side to side on the grass.

"We're almost there!" Rachel cried. "Keep pushing, Kirsty!"

The girls pushed with all their might. Suddenly, the pot turned over and rolled onto its side. Rachel and Kirsty were taken by surprise. They both lost their balance and landed on the grass with a thump.

"Look!" Kirsty whispered, breathing hard.

A small shower of sparkling red dust had flown out of the pot. Rachel and Kirsty gasped with surprise. The dust hung in the air above them. And there, right in the middle of the glittering cloud, was a tiny, winged girl.

Rachel and Kirsty watched in wonder as the tiny girl fluttered in the sunlight. Her delicate wings sparkled with all the colors of the rainbow.

"Oh, Rachel!" Kirsty whispered. "It's a fairy. . . ."

Fairy Magic

The fairy flew over Rachel's and Kirsty's head. Her short, silky dress was the color of ripe strawberries. Red crystal earrings glowed in her ears. Her golden hair was braided with tiny red roses, and she wore crimson slippers on her little feet.

The fairy waved her scarlet wand, and a shower of sparkling red fairy dust

floated softly down to the ground. Where the dust landed, all kinds of red flowers appeared with a *pop!*

Rachel and Kirsty watched, openmouthed. This really and truly *was* a fairy.

"This is like a dream," Rachel said.

"I always believed in fairies," Kirsty whispered back. "But I never thought I'd ever *see* one!"

The fairy flew toward them. "Oh, thank you *so* much!" she called in a tiny voice. "I'm free at last!" She glided down and landed on Kirsty's hand.

Kirsty gasped. The fairy felt lighter and softer than a butterfly.

"I was beginning to think I'd *never* get out of that pot!" the fairy said.

Kirsty wanted to ask the fairy so
many things. But she didn't know
where to start.

"Tell me your names, quickly," said
the fairy. She fluttered up into the air
again. "There's so much to be done,
and we must get started right away."

Rachel wondered what the fairy meant. "I'm Rachel," she said.

"And I'm Kirsty," said Kirsty. "But who are *you*?"

"I'm the Red Rainbow Fairy — but you can call me Ruby," the fairy replied.

"Ruby . . ." Kirsty breathed. "A Rainbow Fairy . . ." She and Rachel stared at each other in excitement. This really *was* magic!

"Yes," said Ruby. "And I have six sisters: Amber, Sunny, Fern, Sky, Inky, and Heather. One for each color of the rainbow, you see."

"What do Rainbow Fairies do?"
Rachel asked.

Ruby flew over and landed lightly on
Rachel's hand. "It's our job to put all the
different colors into Fairyland," she
explained.

"So why were you shut up inside
that old pot?" asked Rachel.

"And where are your sisters?" Kirsty
added.

Ruby's golden wings drooped. Her
eyes filled with tiny, sparkling tears.
"I don't know," she said. "Something
terrible has happened in Fairyland. We
really need your help!"

Fairies in Danger

Kirsty stared down at Ruby, sitting sadly on Rachel's hand. "Of course we'll help you!" she said.

"Just tell us how," added Rachel.

Ruby wiped the tears from her eyes. "Thank you!" she said. "But first I must show you the terrible thing that has

happened. Follow me — as quickly as
you can!" She flew into the
air, her wings shimmering
in the sunshine.

Rachel and Kirsty
followed Ruby across the
clearing. The fairy
danced ahead of
them, glowing like
a crimson flame. She
stopped at a small
pond under a
weeping willow tree.
"Look! I can *show*
you what happened
yesterday," she said.

Ruby flew over the
pond and scattered another shower of

sparkling fairy dust with her tiny, red wand. All at once, the water lit up with a strange, silver light. It bubbled and fizzed, and then became still. With wide eyes, Rachel and Kirsty watched as a picture appeared in the water. It was like looking through a window into another land! "Oh, Rachel, look!" said Kirsty.

A river of the brightest blue ran swiftly past hills of the greenest green. Scattered

on the hillsides were red-and-white
toadstool houses. And on top of the
highest hill stood a silver palace with
four pink towers.

The towers were so high, their points
were almost hidden by the fluffy white
clouds that floated past.

Hundreds of fairies were making their
way toward the palace. Some were
walking and others were flying. Rachel
and Kirsty could see goblins, elves, and
pixies, too. Everyone seemed very
excited.

"Yesterday was the day of the
Fairyland Midsummer Ball," Ruby
explained. She flew over the pond and
pointed with her wand at a spot in the
middle of the scene. "There I am, with
my Rainbow sisters."

Kirsty and Rachel looked closely at
where Ruby was pointing. They saw
seven fairies, each dressed prettily in
her own rainbow color. Wherever

they flew, they left a trail of fairy dust behind them.

"The Midsummer Ball is *very* special," Ruby went on. "And my sisters and I are always in charge of sending out invitations."

The front doors of the palace slowly opened to the sound of tinkling music.

"Here come King Oberon and Queen Titania," said Ruby. "The Fairy King and Queen. They are about to begin the ball."

Kirsty and Rachel watched as the king and queen stepped through the doors. The king wore a splendid golden coat and crown. His queen wore a silver

dress and a tiara that sparkled with
diamonds. Everyone cheered loudly. After a
while, the king signaled for quiet. "Fairies
and friends," he began. "We are very glad
to see you all here. Welcome to the Midsummer Ball!"

The fairies clapped their hands and
cheered again. A band of green frogs in
purple suits started to play their
instruments, and the dancing began.

Suddenly, a gray mist filled the room. Kirsty and Rachel watched in alarm as all the fairies started to shiver. Then a loud, chilly voice shouted out, "Stop the music!"

The band fell silent. Everyone looked scared. A tall, bony figure was pushing his way through the crowd. He was dressed all in white, and there were tiny icicles on his white hair and beard. But his face was red and angry.

"Who's that?" Rachel asked with a shiver. Ice had begun to form around the edge of the pond.

"It's Jack Frost," said Ruby. She shivered, too.

In the watery picture Jack Frost glared at the seven Rainbow Fairies. "Why

wasn't I invited to the Midsummer Ball?"
he asked coldly.

The Rainbow Fairies gasped in
horror. . . .

Ruby looked up and smiled sadly at
Rachel and Kirsty. "Yes, we forgot to invite

Jack Frost," she said, and looked back at the pond.

They watched as the Fairy Queen stepped forward. "You are more than welcome, Jack Frost," she said. "Please stay and enjoy the ball."

But Jack Frost looked even more
angry. "Too late!" he hissed. "You
forgot to invite me!" He turned and
pointed a thin, icy finger at the
Rainbow Fairies.

"You will not forget this!" he went on.

"My spell will banish the Rainbow Fairies to the seven corners of the human world. From this day on, Fairyland will be without color — forever!"

Jack Frost's Spell

As Rachel and Kirsty kept watching the pond's surface, they saw Jack Frost cast his spell. A great, icy wind began to blow. It picked up the seven Rainbow Fairies and spun them up into the darkening sky. The other fairies could only watch in dismay.

Jack Frost turned to the king and queen. "Your Rainbow Fairies will be

trapped far away. They will be all alone, and they will never return." With that, he walked away, leaving only a trail of icy footprints behind.

Quickly, the Fairy Queen stepped forward and lifted her silver wand. "Jack Frost's magic is very powerful. I cannot undo it completely," she shouted, as the wind howled and rushed around

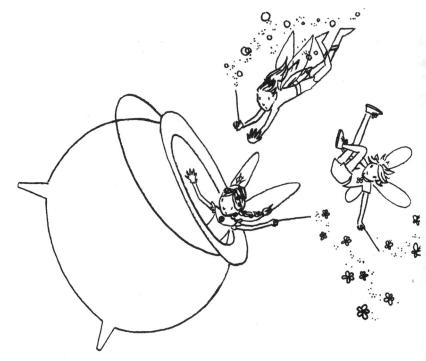

her. "But I can guide the Rainbow Fairies to a place where they will be safe until they are rescued!"

The queen pointed her wand at the gray sky overhead. A black pot came spinning through the stormy clouds. It flew toward the Rainbow Fairies. One by one, the Rainbow Fairies tumbled into the pot.

"May this pot at the end of the rainbow keep our Rainbow Fairies together and safe," the queen called. "And take them to Rainspell Island!"

As Rachel, Kirsty, and Ruby watched, the pot flew out of sight. It disappeared behind a dark cloud. And the bright colors of Fairyland began to fade, until the beautiful land looked like an old black-and-white photograph.

"Oh, no!" Kirsty gasped. "All the color is gone." Then the image in the pond vanished.

"So the Fairy Queen cast her *own* spell!" Rachel said. She was bursting with questions. "She put you and your sisters in the pot, and sent you to Rainspell Island?"

Ruby nodded. "Our queen knew that

we would be safe here," she said. "We
know Rainspell well. It is a place full of
magic."

"But where are your sisters?" Kirsty
asked. "They were in the pot, too."

Ruby looked upset. "Jack Frost's magic
was very strong," she said. "The wind
from his spell blew my sisters right out of

the pot. We were still spinning through the sky, and all at once they were gone." Ruby shook her head. "I was at the bottom, so I was safe. But I was trapped when the pot landed upside down. In the dark, I was frightened and alone. My fairy magic wouldn't even work!"

"So are your sisters somewhere on Rainspell?" Kirsty asked.

Ruby nodded. "Yes, but I think they're scattered all over the island. I'm sure Jack Frost's spell has trapped them, too." She flew toward Kirsty and landed on her shoulder. "That's where you and Rachel come in."

"How?" Rachel asked.

"You found *me*, didn't you?" the fairy went on. "That's because you believe in magic." She flew from Kirsty's shoulder to Rachel's. "So, you could rescue my Rainbow sisters, too! Once we're together, we can bring color back to Fairyland again."

A Visit to Fairyland

"Of course we'll search for your sisters," Kirsty said quickly. "Won't we, Rachel?"

Rachel nodded.

"Oh, thank you!" Ruby said happily.

"But we're only here for a week," Rachel said. "Will that be long enough?"

"We have to get started right away,"

said Ruby. "First, I must take you to
Fairyland to meet our king and
queen. They will be very pleased to
know that you are going to help me
find my sisters."

Rachel and Kirsty stared at Ruby.

"You're taking us to *Fairyland*?"
Kirsty gasped. She could hardly believe
her ears.

"But how will we get there?" Rachel
wanted to know.

"We'll fly," Ruby replied.

"But *we* can't fly!" Rachel pointed
out.

Ruby smiled. She whirled up into
the air over the girls' heads. Then
she swirled her wand above them.
Magic red fairy dust fluttered
down.

Rachel and Kirsty began to feel a bit
strange. Were the trees
getting bigger or were
they getting smaller?

They were getting smaller!
Smaller and smaller and
smaller, until they were
the same size as Ruby.

"I'm tiny!" Rachel laughed.
She was so small, the flowers around
her seemed as big as trees.

Kirsty twisted around to look at her
back. She had wings —
shiny and delicate
as a butterfly's!
Ruby beamed
at them. "Now
you can fly," she
said. "Let's go."

Rachel twitched her shoulders. Her
wings fluttered, and she rose up into the
air. She felt quite wobbly at first. Flying
was not at all like walking!

"Help!" Kirsty yelled, as she shot up
into the air. "I'm not very good at this!"

"Come on," said Ruby, taking their hands. "I'll help you." She led them up out of the meadow.

From the air, Rachel looked down on Rainspell Island. She could see the cottages next to the beach, and the harbor.

"Where *is* Fairyland, Ruby?" Kirsty asked. They were flying higher and higher, up into the clouds.

"It's so far away that no human could ever find it," Ruby said.

They flew on through the clouds for a long, long time. But at last Ruby turned to them and smiled. "We're here," she said. "Luckily, while we're in Fairyland, no time passes in your world. No one will even know you were gone!"

As they flew down from the clouds, Kirsty and Rachel saw places they recognized from the pond picture: the palace, the hillsides with their toadstool houses, the river. But there were no bright colors now. Because of Jack Frost's spell, everything was a drab shade of gray.

A few fairies walked miserably across
the hillsides. Their wings hung limply
down their backs. No one even had the
energy to fly.

Suddenly, one of the fairies glanced up
into the sky. "Look!" she shouted. "It's
Ruby. She's come back!"

At once, the fairies flew up toward
Ruby, Kirsty, and Rachel. They circled
around Ruby, looking much happier,
and asking lots of questions.

"Have you come from Rainspell,
Ruby?"

"Where are the other Rainbow
Fairies?"

"Who are your friends?"

"First, we must see the king and
queen. Then I will tell you
everything!" Ruby promised.

King Oberon and Queen Titania
were seated on their thrones. Their
palace was as gray and gloomy as
everything else in Fairyland. But they
smiled warmly when Ruby arrived with
Rachel and Kirsty.

"Welcome back, Ruby," the queen
said. "We have missed you."

"Your Majesties, I have found two
humans who believe in magic!" Ruby
announced. "These are my new friends,
Kirsty and Rachel."

Quickly, Ruby explained what had
happened to the other Rainbow Fairies.
She told everyone how Rachel and
Kirsty had rescued her.

"You have our thanks," the king
told them. "Our Rainbow Fairies are
very special to us."

"And will you help us to find Ruby's Rainbow sisters?" the queen asked.

"Yes, we will," Kirsty said.

"But how will we know where to look?" Rachel asked.

"The trick is not to look too hard," said Queen Titania. "Don't worry. As you enjoy the rest of your vacation, the magic you need to find each Rainbow Fairy will find *you*. Just wait and see."

King Oberon rubbed his beard thoughtfully. "You have six days of your vacation left, and six fairies to find," he said. "A fairy each day. That's a lot of fairy-finding. You will need some special help." He nodded at one of his footmen, a plump frog in a buttoned-up jacket.

The frog hopped over to Rachel and
Kirsty and handed them each a tiny,
silver bag.

"The bags contain magic tools," the
queen told them. "Don't look inside

them yet. Open them only when you
really need to, and you will find
something to help you." She smiled at
Kirsty and Rachel.

"Look!" shouted another frog footman suddenly. "Ruby is beginning to fade!"

Rachel and Kirsty looked at Ruby in horror. The fairy was growing paler

before their eyes. Her lovely dress was
no longer red, but pink, and her golden
hair was turning white.

"Jack Frost's magic is still at work,"
said the king, looking worried. "We
cannot undo his spell until the Rainbow
Fairies are all together again."

"Quickly, Ruby!" urged the queen.
"You must return to Rainspell at once."

Ruby, Kirsty, and Rachel rose into the
air, their wings fluttering.

"Don't worry!" Kirsty called, as they
flew higher. "We'll come back with all
the Rainbow Fairies very soon!"

"Good luck!" called the king and queen.

Rachel and Kirsty watched Ruby
worriedly as they all flew off together. As
they got farther away from Fairyland,

Ruby's color began to return. Soon she was bright and sparkling again. The three girls reached Rainspell at last. Ruby led Rachel and Kirsty to the clearing in the woods, and they landed next to the old, black pot. Then Ruby scattered fairy dust over Rachel and Kirsty. There was a puff of glittering red smoke, and the two girls shot up to their normal size again. Rachel wriggled her shoulders. Yes, her wings were gone.

"Oh, I really *loved* being a fairy," Kirsty said.

They watched as Ruby sprinkled her magic dust over the old, black pot.

"What are you doing?" Rachel asked.

"Jack Frost's magic means that I can't help you look for my sisters," Ruby replied sadly. "If I try, I might fade away completely. So I will wait for you here, in the pot at the end of the rainbow."

Suddenly, the pot began to move. It rolled across the grass and stopped under the weeping willow tree. The tree's branches hung right down to the ground.

"The pot will be hidden under that tree," Ruby explained. "I'll be safe there."

"We'd better start looking for the other Rainbow Fairies," Rachel said to Kirsty. "Where shall we start?"

Ruby shook her head. "Remember what the queen said," she told them. "The magic will come to you." She flew over and sat on the edge of the pot. Then she pushed aside one of the willow branches and waved at Rachel and Kirsty. "Good-bye, and good luck!"

"We'll be back soon, Ruby," Kirsty promised.

"We're going to find all of your
Rainbow sisters," Rachel said firmly.
"Just you wait and see!"

Amber

the Orange
Fairy

Dedicated to Fiona Waters,
who has loved fairies
all her life

Special thanks to
Narinder Dhami

A Very Unusual Shell

"What a beautiful day!" Rachel Walker shouted, staring up at the blue sky. She and her friend Kirsty Tate were running along Rainspell Island's yellow, sandy beach. Their parents walked a little way behind them.

"It's a *magical* day," Kirsty added. The two friends smiled at each other.

Rachel and Kirsty had come to
Rainspell Island for their vacations.
But they soon found out it really
was a magical place!

As they ran, they passed tide pools
that sparkled like jewels in the sunshine.

Rachel spotted a little *splash!* in one of
the pools. "There's something in there,
Kirsty!" She pointed. "Let's go look."

The girls jogged over to the pool and
crouched down to see.

Kirsty's heart thumped as she gazed into the crystal-clear water. "What is it?" she asked.

Suddenly, the water rippled. A little brown crab scuttled sideways across the sandy bottom and disappeared under a rock.

Kirsty felt disappointed. "I thought it might be another Rainbow Fairy," she said.

"So did I." Rachel sighed. "Never mind. We'll keep looking."

"Of course we will," Kirsty agreed. Then she put her finger to her lips as their parents came up behind them. *"Shhh."*

Kirsty and Rachel had a big secret. They were helping to find the seven missing Rainbow Fairies. Jack Frost put a wicked spell on the fairies and trapped them on Rainspell Island. The Rainbow Fairies made Fairyland bright and colorful. Until they were all found, Fairyland would be dark and gray.

Rachel looked at the shimmering blue sea. "Do you want to go swimming?" she asked.

But Kirsty wasn't listening. She was shading her eyes with her hand and looking farther along the beach. "Look over there, Rachel — by those rocks," she said.

Then Rachel could see it, too — something glittering and sparkling in the sunshine. "Wait for me!" she

called, as Kirsty hurried down the
beach.

When they saw what it was, the two
friends sighed in disappointment.

"It's just the wrapper from a
chocolate bar," Rachel said sadly. She

bent down and picked up the shiny, purple foil.

Kirsty thought for a moment. "Do you remember what the Fairy Queen told us?" she asked.

Rachel nodded. *"Let the magic come to you,"* she said. "You're right, Kirsty. We should just enjoy our vacation, and wait for the magic to happen. After all, that's how we found Ruby in the pot at the end of the rainbow, isn't it?" She put

her beach bag down on the sand.
"Come on — race you to the water!"

They rushed into the water. The sea
was cold and salty, but the sun felt warm
on their backs. They waved at their
parents, sitting on the sand, and splashed
around in the waves until they got
goose bumps.

"Ow!" Kirsty gasped as they paddled
out of the water. "I just stepped on
something sharp."

"It might have been a shell,"
said Rachel. "There are lots
of them around here." She
picked up a pale pink one
and showed it to Kirsty.

"Let's see how many we can find,"
Kirsty said.

The two girls walked along the beach looking for shells. They found long, thin, blue shells and tiny, round, white shells. Soon their hands were full. They had walked right around the curve of the bay. Rachel looked over her shoulder and a sudden gust of wind whipped her hair across her face. "Look how far we've come," she said. Kirsty stopped. The wind blew at her back and made goose bumps stand out on her arms.

"It's getting cold now," she said.
"Should we go back?"

"Yes, it must be almost lunchtime,"
said Rachel.

The two girls began to walk back
along the beach. They'd only gone a
few steps when the wind suddenly
stopped.

"That's funny," said Kirsty. "It's not
windy here at all."

They looked back and saw perfect
little swirls of sand being lifted by the

wind. "Oh!" said Rachel, and the two
friends looked at each other in
excitement.

"It's magic," Kirsty whispered. "It just
has to be!"

They walked back to where they had
been, and the breeze swirled around
their legs again. Then the golden sand
at their feet began to drift gently to one
side, as if invisible hands were pushing it
away. A large scallop shell appeared. It
was much bigger than the other shells
on the beach. It was a light peach color
with soft orange streaks, and it was
tightly closed.

Quickly, the girls kneeled down on the
sand, dropping the little shells from their
hands. Kirsty was just about to pick up

the scallop shell when Rachel put out her hand. "Listen," she whispered.

They both listened hard.

Rachel smiled when she heard the sound again.

Inside the shell, a tiny voice hummed softly. . . .

The Magic Feather

Very carefully, Rachel picked up the shell. It felt warm and smooth.

The humming stopped at once. "I should not be scared," said the tiny voice. "I just have to be brave, and help will come very soon."

Hummm...

83

Kirsty put her face close to the shell. "Hello," she whispered. "Is there a fairy in there?"

"Yes!" cried the voice. "I'm Amber the Orange Fairy! Can you get me out of here?"

"Of course we will," Kirsty promised. "My name is Kirsty, and my friend Rachel is here, too." She looked up at Rachel, her eyes shining. "We've found another Rainbow Fairy!"

"Quick," Rachel said. "Let's get the shell open." She took hold of the scallop shell and tried to pull the two halves apart. Nothing happened.

"Try again," said Kirsty. She and Rachel each grabbed one half of the shell and tugged. But the shell stayed tightly shut.

"What's happening?" Amber asked. She sounded worried.

"We can't open the shell," Kirsty said. "But we'll think of something." She turned to Rachel. "If we find a piece of driftwood, maybe we can use it to pry open the shell."

Rachel glanced around the beach. "I don't see any driftwood," she said. "We could try tapping the shell on a rock."

"But that might hurt Amber," Kirsty pointed out.

Suddenly, Rachel remembered something. "What about the magic bags the Fairy Queen gave us?" she said.

"Of course!" Kirsty cried. She put her face close to the shell again.

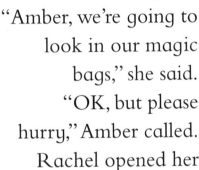

"Amber, we're going to look in our magic bags," she said.

"OK, but please hurry," Amber called. Rachel opened her beach bag. The two magic bags were hidden under her towel. One of the bags was glowing with a golden light. Carefully, Rachel pulled it out. "Look," she whispered to Kirsty. "This one is all lit up."

"Open it, quick," Kirsty whispered back.

As Rachel untied the bag, a fountain of glittering sparks flew out.

"What's inside?" Kirsty asked, gently putting down the shell.

Rachel slid her hand into the bag. She could feel something light and soft. She pulled it out, scattering sparkles everywhere. It was a shimmering golden feather.

Kirsty and Rachel stared at the feather.

"It's really pretty," said Kirsty. "But what are we going to *do* with it?"

"I don't know," Rachel replied. She tried to use the feather to push the two halves of the shell apart. But the feather just curled up in her hand. "Maybe we should ask Amber."

"Amber, we've looked in the magic bags," Kirsty said, "and we found a feather."

"Oh, good!" Amber said happily from inside the shell. "That's wonderful news!"

"But we don't know what to do with it," Rachel added.

Amber laughed. It sounded like the tinkle of a tiny bell. "You tickle the shell, of course!" she said.

"Do you think that will work?" Rachel said to Kirsty.

"Let's give it a try," Kirsty said.

Rachel began to tickle the shell with
the feather. At first nothing happened.
Then they heard a soft, gritty chuckle,

followed by a tinkly giggle from inside
the shell.

Then another chuckle, and another.
Slowly, the two halves of the shell began
to open.

"It's working." Kirsty gasped. "Keep
tickling, Rachel!"

The shell was laughing hard now.
The two halves opened wider. . . .
And there, sitting inside the smooth,
peach-colored shell, was Amber the
Orange Fairy.

A Stranger in the Pot

"I'm free!" Amber cried joyfully.

She shot out of the shell and up into the air, her wings fluttering in a rainbow-colored blur. Orange fairy dust floated down around Kirsty and Rachel. It turned into orange bubbles as it fell. One of the bubbles landed on Rachel's arm and burst with a tiny *pop!*

"The bubbles smell like oranges!" Rachel said with a smile.

Amber spun through the sky, turning cartwheels one after the other. "Thank you!" she called. Then she swooped down toward Rachel and Kirsty.

She wore a shiny orange leotard and tall boots. Her brown hair was held in a high ponytail, tied with a band of peach blossoms. In her hand was an orange wand tipped with gold.

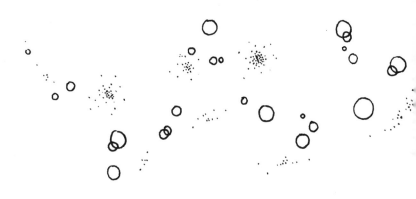

"I'm so glad you found me!" Amber
shouted. She landed on Rachel's
shoulder, then cartwheeled lightly across
to Kirsty's. "But who are you? And
where are my Rainbow sisters? And
what's happening in Fairyland? How
am I going to get back there?"

She was talking so fast that Kirsty and
Rachel couldn't get a word in.

Suddenly, Amber stopped. She floated down and landed softly on Rachel's hand. "I'm sorry," she said with a smile. "But I haven't had anyone to talk to. I've been trapped in that shell ever since Jack Frost's spell banished us from Fairyland. How did you know where to find me?"

"Kirsty and I promised your sister Ruby that we would look for all the Rainbow Fairies," Rachel told her.

"Ruby?" Amber's face lit up. She spun around on Rachel's hand. "You've found Ruby?"

"Yes, she's safe now," Rachel said. "She's in the pot at the end of the rainbow."

Amber did a happy backflip. "Please take me to her!" she begged.

"I'll ask our parents if we can go for a walk," Kirsty said. And she ran off across the beach.

"Do you know what's happening in Fairyland?" Amber asked Rachel.

Rachel nodded. She and Kirsty had flown to Fairyland with Ruby. Ruby had used her wand to shrink them to fairy size, and she had given them magical fairy wings. "King Oberon and Queen Titania miss you very much," Rachel told Amber. "With no color, Fairyland is a sad place."

Amber's wings drooped.

Kirsty was hurrying back toward them. "Mom said we can go for a walk," she panted.

"Well, what are we waiting for? Let's go!" Amber called. She flew up and did a somersault in midair. Rachel pulled their shorts, T-shirts, and sneakers out of her beach bag and both girls put them on. "Rachel, could you bring my shell?" Amber asked. Rachel looked surprised. "Yes, if you want," she said.

Amber nodded. "It's really comfy," she explained. "It will make a lovely bed for me and my sisters."

Rachel put the shell in her beach bag, and they set off, with Amber sitting cross-legged on Kirsty's shoulder.

"My wings are a bit stiff after being in the shell for so long," she told them. "I don't think I can fly very far yet."

The girls followed the path to the clearing in the woods where the pot at the end of the rainbow was hidden.

"Here we are," said Rachel. "The pot is right over there." She stopped. The pot was where they'd left it — under the

weeping willow tree. But climbing out
of it was a big, green frog.

"Oh, no!" Rachel gasped. She and
Kirsty stared at the frog in horror.

Where was Ruby?

Home Sweet Home

Rachel dashed forward and grabbed the
frog around his plump, green tummy.

The frog turned his head and glared
at her, his eyes bulging. "And what do
you think *you're* doing?" he croaked.

Rachel was so shocked, she let go of
the frog. He hopped away from her,
looking very annoyed.

"It's a talking frog!" Kirsty gasped, her eyes wide. "And it looks like it's wearing glasses. . . ."

"Bertram!" Amber flew down from Kirsty's shoulder. "I didn't know it was you."

Bertram bowed his head as Amber hugged him. "Thank goodness you're safe, Miss Amber!" he said happily. "And may I say, it's very good to see you again."

Amber beamed at Rachel and Kirsty. "Bertram isn't an ordinary frog, you know," she explained. "He's one of King Oberon's footmen. He works closely with the king and queen."

"Oh, yes!" said Kirsty. "I remember now. We saw the frog footmen when we went to Fairyland with Ruby."

"But they were wearing uniforms then," Rachel added.

"Excuse me, miss, but a frog in a uniform would *not* be a good idea on Rainspell Island," Bertram pointed out.

"It's much better if I look like an ordinary frog."

"But what are you doing here, Bertram?" asked Amber. "And where's Ruby?"

"Don't worry, Miss Amber," Bertram replied. "Miss Ruby is safe in the pot." He suddenly looked very stern. "King Oberon sent me to Rainspell. The Cloud Fairies spotted Jack Frost's goblins sneaking out of Fairyland. We think he has sent them here to stop you from finding the Rainbow Fairies."

Kirsty felt a shiver run down down her spine. "Jack Frost's goblins?" she said.

"They're his servants," Amber explained. Her wings trembled

and she looked very scared. "They want to keep Fairyland cold and gray!"

"Never fear, Miss Amber!" Bertram croaked. "I'm here to look after you and keep the Rainbow Fairies safe."

Suddenly, a shower of red fairy dust shot out of the pot. Ruby fluttered out. "I heard voices," she shouted joyfully.

"Amber! I *knew* it was you!"

"Ruby!" Amber called. And then she cartwheeled through the air toward her sister.

Rachel and Kirsty watched as the two
fairies flew into each other's arms. The
air around them fizzed with little red
flowers and orange bubbles.

"Thank you, Kirsty
and Rachel," said Ruby.
She and Amber floated
down to them, holding
hands. "It's so good to
have Amber back
safely."

"What about you?"
Rachel asked. "Have you been
OK in the pot?"

Ruby nodded. "I'm fine now that
Bertram is here," she replied. "And I've
been making the pot into a fairy home.
We can stay there until all our fairy
sisters are found."

"I brought my shell with me," Amber said. "It will make a lovely bed for us. Could you show her, Rachel?"

Rachel put her bag down on the grass and took the peach-colored shell out of it.

"It's beautiful," said Ruby. Then she smiled at Rachel and Kirsty. "Would you like to come and see our new home?" she asked.

"But the pot's much too small for Kirsty and me to fit inside," Rachel began. Then she started to tingle with excitement. "Oh! Are you going to make us fairy size again?"

Ruby nodded. She and Amber flew over the girls' heads, showering them with fairy dust. Rachel and Kirsty started to shrink, just as they had

before. Soon they were the same size as Ruby and Amber.

"I *love* being a fairy," Kirsty said happily. She twisted around to look at her silvery wings.

"Me, too," Rachel agreed. She was getting used to seeing flowers as tall as trees!

Bertram hopped over to the pot. "I'll wait outside," he croaked.

"Come this way," said Ruby. She took Rachel's hand, and Amber took Kirsty's. Then the fairies led them toward the pot.

Rachel and Kirsty fluttered through

the air, dodging a butterfly that was
as big as they were. Its wings
felt like velvet as
they brushed
gently past it.

"I'm getting
better at flying!"
Kirsty said as she
landed neatly on
the edge of the pot.
She looked down eagerly.

The pot was full of sunlight. There

were little chairs made from twigs tied
with blades of grass. Each chair had a
cushion made from a soft, red berry.
Rugs of bright green leaves covered
the floor.

"Should we bring in the shell?" asked
Rachel.

The others thought this was a very
good idea. When they flew out of the
pot, Bertram was already pushing the
shell across the grass toward them.

"Here you are," he croaked.

The shell seemed very heavy now that Rachel and Kirsty were the same size as Ruby and Amber. But Bertram helped them lift it into the pot. Soon the shell bed sat neatly inside.

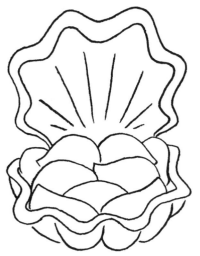

Ruby lined it with sweet-smelling rose petals.

"The pot looks lovely," Rachel said.

"I wish I could live here, too!" said Kirsty.

Ruby turned to her sister. "Do *you* like it, Amber?" she asked.

"It's beautiful," Amber replied. "It reminds me of our house back in Fairyland. I wish I could see Fairyland again. I miss it so much."

Ruby smiled. "Well, we can't go back to Fairyland for good until we're all together," she explained. "But I can *show* you Fairyland. Follow me!"

Bertram was still on guard next to the pot when they flew outside again. "Where are

you going, Miss Ruby?" he croaked.

"To the magic pond," Ruby replied. "Come with us." She sprinkled her magic dust over Rachel and Kirsty. Quickly, they grew back to their normal size. They went over to the pond.

Ruby flew above the water, scattering fairy dust. Just like before, a picture began to appear.

"Fairyland!" Amber cried, gazing into
the water.

Rachel and Kirsty watched, too.
Fairyland still looked sad and chilly. The

palace, the toadstool houses, the flowers, and the trees were all icy and gray.

Suddenly, a cold breeze rippled the surface of the the water, and the picture started to fade.

"What's happening?" Kirsty whispered.

Everyone stared down at the pond.
Another picture was taking shape — a
thin, grinning face with frosty white
hair and icicles hanging from his beard.

"Jack Frost!" Ruby gasped in horror.
As she spoke, the air turned icy cold
and the edges of the pool began to
freeze.

"What's happening?" Rachel asked,
shivering.

Bertram hopped forward. "This is bad
news," he said. "It means that Jack
Frost's goblins must be close by!"

Goblin Alert!

Rachel and Kirsty felt shivers run down their spines as the whole pond froze over. Jack Frost's grinning face faded away.

"Follow me," ordered Bertram. He hopped over to a large bush. "We'll hide here."

"Maybe we should go back to the pot," said Ruby.

"Not if the goblins are close by,"
Bertram replied. "We can't let them
know where the pot is."

The two girls crouched down behind
the bush next to Bertram. Ruby and
Amber sat very still on Kirsty's shoulder.
It was getting colder and colder. Rachel
and Kirsty couldn't stop their teeth from
chattering.

"What are the goblins like?" Rachel asked.

"They're bigger than us," said Amber. She was trembling with fear.

"And they have mean faces and long noses and big feet," Ruby added, holding her sister's hand for comfort.

"Hush, Miss Ruby," Bertram croaked. "I hear something."

Rachel and Kirsty listened. Suddenly, Rachel saw a long-nosed shadow dash across the clearing toward them. She grabbed Kirsty's arm. They were peering out of the bush when the leaves rustled right next to them. The two girls almost jumped out of their skin.

"Hey!" said a gruff voice, sounding very close. "What do you think you're doing?" Rachel and Kirsty held their breath.

"Nothing," said another gruff voice, rudely. "Goblins!" Amber whispered in Kirsty's ear.

"You stepped on my toe," said the first goblin angrily.

"No, I didn't," snapped the other goblin.

"Yes, you did! Keep your big feet to yourself!"

"Well, at least my nose isn't as big as yours!"

The bush shook even more. It
sounded like the goblins were pushing
and shoving each other.

"Get out of my way!" one of them
shouted. "Ow!"

"That'll teach you to push *me*!" yelled
the other one.

Rachel and Kirsty looked at each
other in alarm. What if the goblins
found them there?

"Come on," puffed one of the goblins. "Jack Frost will be really angry if we don't find these fairies. You know he wants us to keep them from getting back to Fairyland."

"Well, they're not here, are they?" grumbled the other. "Let's try somewhere else."

The voices died away. The leaves stopped rustling. And suddenly, the air felt warm again. There was a cracking sound as the frozen pond began to melt.

"They're gone," Bertram croaked. "Quick, we must get back to the pot."

They all hurried across the clearing. The pot stood under the weeping willow tree, just as before.

"I'll stay outside in case the goblins come back," Bertram began. But a shout from Kirsty stopped them all in their tracks.

"Look!" she cried. "The pot's frozen over!"

Kirsty was right. The top of the pot was covered with a thick sheet of ice. No one, not even a fairy, could get inside.

Bertram to the Rescue

"Oh, no!" Ruby gasped. "The goblins must have been really close. Thank goodness they didn't discover the pot."

She flew over to the pot with Amber right behind her. They drummed on the ice with their tiny fists. But it was too thick for them to break through.

"Should *we* try, Rachel?" asked Kirsty.

"Maybe we could smash the ice with a stick."

But Bertram had another idea. "Stand back, please, everyone," he said.

The girls moved to the edge of the clearing. Ruby sat on Kirsty's hand, and Amber flew over to Rachel. They all watched.

Suddenly, Bertram took a mighty hop forward. He jumped right at the sheet of ice, kicking out with his webbed feet. But the ice did not break. "Let's try again," he panted.

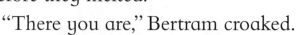

He jumped forward
again and hit the ice.
This time, there was a
loud cracking sound. After
one more jump, the ice
shattered into little pieces.
Some of it fell inside the pot.
Rachel and Kirsty rushed over
to fish out the pieces of ice
before they melted.

"There you are," Bertram croaked.

"Thank you, Bertram," Ruby called.
She and Amber flew down and hugged
the frog.

Bertram looked pleased. "Just doing
my job, Miss Ruby," he said. "You and
Miss Amber must stay very close to the
pot from now on. It's dangerous for you
to go too far."

"We've got to say
good-bye to our friends
first," Amber told him.
She flew into the air and
did a backflip, smiling at
Rachel and Kirsty. "Thank you
a thousand times."

"We'll see you again soon," said
Rachel.

"When we've found your next
Rainbow sister," Kirsty added.

"Good luck!" said Ruby. "We'll be
waiting here for you. Come on,
Amber." She took her
sister's hand, and they
flew over to the pot.

The two fairies turned
to wave at the girls.
Then they disappeared inside.

"Don't worry," Bertram said. "I'll look after them."

"We know you will," Rachel said as she picked up her beach bag. She and Kirsty walked out of the woods. "I'm glad Ruby isn't on her own anymore," said Rachel. "Now she has Amber *and* Bertram."

"I didn't like those goblins," Kirsty said with a shudder. "I hope they don't come back again."

The girls made their way back to the beach. Their parents were packing up their towels. Rachel's dad saw Rachel and Kirsty coming down the path and went to meet them. "You've been gone a long time." He smiled. "We were just coming to look for you."

"Are we going home now?" Rachel asked.

Mr. Walker nodded. "It's very strange," he said. "It's suddenly turned quite chilly."

As he spoke, a cold breeze swirled around Rachel and Kirsty. The friends shivered and looked up at the sky. The sun had disappeared behind a thick, black cloud. The trees swayed in the wind, and the leaves rustled as if they were whispering to one another.

"Jack Frost's goblins are still here!" Kirsty whispered.

"You're right," Rachel agreed. "Let's hope Bertram can keep Ruby and Amber safe while we look for the other Rainbow Fairies."

Kirsty nodded and smiled at Rachel. They still had five fairies to find. It would take some magic and a lot of work, but she was sure they could do it together!

Sunny
the Yellow
Fairy

Previously published as *Saffron the Yellow Fairy*

To the fairies at the
bottom of my garden

Special thanks to
Sue Bentley

A Very Big Bee

"Over here, Kirsty!" called Rachel Walker. Kirsty Tate ran across one of the emerald-green fields that covered this part of Rainspell Island. Buttercups and daisies dotted the grass.

"Don't go too far!" Kirsty's mom called. She and Kirsty's dad were climbing over a fence at the edge of the field.

Kirsty caught up with her friend.

"What did you find, Rachel? Is it another Rainbow Fairy?" she asked hopefully.

"I don't know." Rachel was standing on the bank of a rippling stream. "I thought I heard something."

Kirsty's face lit up. "Maybe there's a fairy in the stream?"

Rachel nodded. She knelt down on the soft grass and put her ear close to the water.

Kirsty crouched down, too, and listened really hard.

The sun glittered on the water as it splashed over big, shiny pebbles. Tiny rainbows flashed and sparkled — red, orange, yellow, green, blue, indigo, and violet.

And then the girls heard a tiny
bubbling voice. "Follow me. . . ." it
gurgled. "Follow me. . . ."

"Oh!" Rachel gasped. "Did you
hear that?"

"Yes," said Kirsty, her eyes wide. "It
must be a *magic* stream!"

Rachel felt her heart beat fast.

"Maybe the stream will lead us to the
Yellow Fairy," she said.

Rachel and Kirsty had a special
secret. They had promised the King
and Queen of Fairyland they would
find the lost Rainbow Fairies. Jack
Frost's spell had hidden the Rainbow
Fairies on Rainspell Island. Fairyland
would be cold and gray until all seven
fairies had been found and returned to
their home.

Silver fish darted in and out of the
bright green weeds at the bottom of the
stream. "Follow us, follow us. . . ." they
whispered in tinkling voices.

Rachel and Kirsty smiled at each other. Titania, the Fairy Queen, had said that the magic would find them!

Kirsty's parents came up behind the girls and stopped to admire the stream, too. "Which way now?" asked Mr. Tate. "You two seem to know where you're going."

"Let's go this way," Kirsty said, pointing along the bank.

A brilliant bluebird flew up from its perch on a twig. Butterflies as bright as jewels fluttered among the cattails.

"Everything on Rainspell Island is so beautiful," said Kirsty's mom. "I'm glad we still have five days of vacation left!"

Yes, Rachel thought, *and five Rainbow Fairies still to find: Sunny, Fern, Sky, Inky, and Heather!* Ruby the Red Fairy and Amber the Orange Fairy were already safe in the pot at the end of the rainbow, thanks to Rachel and Kirsty.

The girls ran on ahead of Mr. and Mrs. Tate. As they followed the bubbling stream, the sun went behind a big, dark cloud.

A chilly breeze ruffled Kirsty's hair. She noticed that some of the leaves on the trees were turning brown, even though it wasn't autumn. Strange weather like that could only mean one thing. "It looks like Jack Frost's goblins are still  around," she warned Rachel. Whenever the goblins were nearby, everything turned frosty and cold.

Rachel shivered. "Horrible creatures! They'll do anything to stop the Rainbow Fairies from getting back to Fairyland."

The two friends stared anxiously up at the sky. But just then, the sun came out again, warming their shoulders. The girls smiled with relief and continued to follow the bubbling water.

The stream wound through a field covered with green clover. A herd of black-and-white cows was grazing at the water's edge. They looked up with their huge, brown eyes.

"Aren't they cute?" Kirsty asked.
Suddenly, the cows tossed their heads
and ran off toward the
other end of the field.
Rachel and Kirsty
looked at each other
in surprise. What was
going on?
Then they heard a loud
buzzing noise.
A small shape came
whizzing through the air, straight
toward them! Rachel jumped. "It's a
bee!" she gasped.

"Run!" Kirsty cried. "The cows had
the right idea!" Rachel tore through the
meadow with Kirsty right next to her,
their feet pounding the grass.

"Keep running, girls," called Mr. Tate,

catching up with them.
"That bee seems like it's
following us!"

Rachel glanced back
over her shoulder. The bee
was huge, bigger than
any bee she'd ever seen.

"In here, quick!" Mrs. Tate called
from the side of the field. She pulled
open a wooden gate.

They all ran through it, then stopped
to catch their breath. Hopefully, they'd
lost that bee — for good!

"I wonder who lives here," Kirsty
panted. They were standing in a beautiful yard. A path led up to a little cottage
with yellow roses around the door.

Just then, a very strange creature
came out from behind some trees. It
looked like an alien from
outer space!

"Oh!" Rachel
and Kirsty gasped.

The creature lifted
its gloved hands
and removed
its white helmet
to reveal . . . an

old woman! She smiled at them.

"Sorry if I scared you," she said. "I do look a little strange in my beekeeper's suit."

Rachel sighed in relief. It wasn't an alien after all!

"I'm Mrs. Merry," the old lady went on.

"Hello," Rachel said. "I'm Rachel. This is my friend Kirsty."

"And this is my mom and dad," Kirsty added.

Mr. and Mrs. Tate greeted Mrs. Merry. Then Mr. Tate ducked as the huge bee zoomed past his ear. "Watch out!" he said. "It's back!"

"Oh, it's that hiveless queen again," said Mrs. Merry. She flapped her hand at the bee. "Go on, shoo!"

Rachel watched it swoop over a low hedge and disappear.

"That bee chased us all the way here. Why would she do that?" Kirsty asked.

"I don't think she was chasing you, my dear," said Mrs. Merry. "She was just heading this way because she's looking for a hive of her own. But all of my hives already have queens."

"Well, thank goodness she's gone now!" said Mrs. Tate.

"Since you're here, would you like to try some of my honey?" Mrs. Merry asked. Her blue eyes sparkled happily.

"Oh, yes, please," said Rachel.

The others nodded, and they followed

Mrs. Merry across the lawn to a table covered with rows of jars.

Each jar was filled with rich golden honey. Rays of sunlight danced over the jars, making the honey glow.

"Here you are," said Mrs. Merry, spooning some honey onto a pretty yellow plate.

"Thank you," Rachel said politely. She dipped her finger into the little pool of honey and popped it into her mouth. The honey was the most delicious thing she had ever tasted — sweet and smooth.

Then she felt it begin to tingle on her tongue. She looked over at Kirsty. "It tastes all fizzy!" she whispered.

Kirsty dipped her finger into the honey, too. "And look!" she said.

Rachel saw that the honey was twinkling with thousands of tiny, gold sparkles. She grabbed Kirsty's arm. "Do you think this means —"

"Yes," said Kirsty. Her eyes were shining. "Another Rainbow Fairy must be nearby!"

The Magic Hive

"We have to find out where this honey came from!" Rachel said excitedly.

"Yes," Kirsty agreed. "Mom? Can we stay here a bit longer, please?"

"As long as it's OK with Mrs. Merry," Kirsty's mom replied.

Mrs. Merry beamed. "Of course they can stay," she said kindly.

Mr. and Mrs. Tate decided to continue their walk. "Make sure you come back to Dolphin Cottage by lunchtime," Kirsty's mom said. "And be careful!"

"We will," Kirsty promised.

"Come along then, girls." Mrs. Merry set off across the smooth, green lawn.

Rachel and Kirsty followed her to some old and twisted apple trees. Six wooden hives stood underneath.

Kirsty stared at the row of hives. "Which one did the honey we tasted come from?" she asked.

Mrs. Merry looked pleased. "Did you enjoy it? The honey from that hive tastes especially good at the moment."

Rachel and Kirsty grinned at each other.

"I think we might know why," Rachel whispered to Kirsty.

"Yes," Kirsty agreed. "It could be fairy honey!"

"That's the one," Mrs. Merry said proudly, pointing to the very back of the yard. One hive stood there all alone, beneath the tallest apple tree.

As they walked toward the hive, the girls could hear a sleepy buzzing sound. "The bees in this hive are very peaceful nowadays," said Mrs. Merry. "I've never known them to be so happy."

"Can we get a bit closer?" Rachel asked eagerly. She couldn't wait to find out if the hive held a magical secret!

Mrs. Merry looked thoughtful. "I think it's safe, with the bees so quiet," she decided. "But you had better wear a hood like mine, just in case."

She went into a nearby shed and brought out two beekeepers' hoods. "Here you are."

Rachel and Kirsty pulled the hoods
over their heads. It was a bit dark and
stuffy inside, but they could see through
the netting just fine.

They moved closer to the hive. The
soft buzzing sounded almost like music.

"We need to open it and take a look,"
Kirsty whispered to Rachel.

Rachel nodded.

But they couldn't start searching for
the Yellow Fairy with Mrs. Merry there.
Ruby had warned them that no grown-
ups should see the fairies.

Suddenly, Kirsty had an idea. "Mrs.
Merry, could I have a drink of water,
please?" she asked.

"Of course you can, dear," Mrs.
Merry said. "I'll be right back." She
went off toward the cottage.

The girls waited until Mrs. Merry
disappeared inside.

"Quick!" Kirsty spun around. "Let's
open the hive."

Rachel grasped one end of the lid.
Kirsty took hold of the other end. They
pulled hard, and the lid slowly came loose
with a squeaky sound. Strings of golden
honey stretched down from it.

"Watch out. It's very sticky,"
Rachel said.

The girls bent down and laid the
heavy wooden top carefully on the
ground. Kirsty wiped her fingers on the
grass.

"Look!" Rachel whispered as she
stood up.

Kirsty turned to see, and gasped.

A shower of sparkling gold dust shot up out of the hive. It hung in a soft cloud, shimmering and dancing in the sunlight. Fairy dust!

Rachel leaned over and peered down into the hive. A tiny girl was sitting cross-legged on a piece of honeycomb, in the middle of a golden sea of honey.

A bee lay with its head in her lap while she combed its silky hair. Several other bees were waiting their turn, buzzing gently.

"Oh, Kirsty," Rachel whispered. "We've found another Rainbow Fairy!"

Bee Friends

Rachel and Kirsty took off their hoods and stared down into the hive with excitement.

The fairy had bright yellow hair. She wore a necklace of golden raindrops and lots of sparkly golden bracelets. Her T-shirt and shorts were the color of buttercups.

Her delicate wings sparkled with a
thousand shimmering rainbows.

"Oh, thank you for finding me!" the
fairy said in a tinkling voice. "I'm
Sunny the Yellow Fairy."

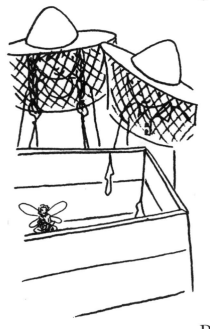

Rachel and
Kirsty introduced
themselves.
"We've met two
of your sisters
already — Ruby
and Amber,"
Kirsty added.
Sunny beamed
happily.
"You've found
Ruby and Amber?"
She stood up, gently
pushing the bee away.

"Yes. They're safe in the pot at the end of the rainbow," Rachel said.

Sunny clapped her tiny hands. "I can't *wait* to see them again." Suddenly, she looked worried. "Have you seen any of Jack Frost's goblins near here?" she asked.

"No, not here," Kirsty said. "But there were some by the pot yesterday."

"We hid behind a bush until they went away," Rachel explained.

"Goblins are scary," Sunny said in a trembling voice. "I've been safe from them here in the hive, with my bee friends."

Rachel felt very sorry for Sunny. "It's all right. King Oberon sent one of his frog footmen to look after you and your sisters."

Sunny cheered up. "I've been really worried about finding my sisters. Jack Frost's magic is so cold and strong."

"It won't be long now," Kirsty said. "We are going to find Fern, Sky, Inky, and Heather, too, aren't we, Rachel?"

"Yes. We promised," Rachel agreed.

"Oh, thank you!" Sunny said. She threw out her arms and gave a shake of her sparkling wings.

Fairy dust rose into the air and drifted down around Rachel and Kirsty. Where it landed, bright yellow butterflies appeared, with tiny fluttering wings.

A large bee crawled out of one of the waxy openings in the honeycomb next to Sunny.

"This is my new friend, Queenie," said Sunny. She put her arms around the bee's neck and kissed the top of her furry head.

Queenie buzzed softly.

"She says hello," said Sunny.

"Hello, Queenie," Kirsty and Rachel said together.

Sunny picked up her tiny comb and began to comb Queenie's shiny hair. Another bee buzzed angrily.

"Don't worry, Petal, I'll comb your hair next," Sunny said.

Rachel and Kirsty looked at each other in dismay.

"What if Sunny wants to stay with Queenie and the other bees?" Kirsty whispered.

"Sunny, you have to come with us!" Rachel burst out. "Or Fairyland will never get its colors back! It will take all seven of the Rainbow sisters to undo Jack Frost's spell."

Forgetful Fairy

"Yes, you're right! We have to break Jack Frost's spell!" Sunny cried. She jumped to her feet and picked up her wand.

Suddenly, an icy wind swept by. Something crunched under Kirsty's feet. There was a small patch of frost on the grass. Rachel shivered as something cold brushed against her cheek.

173

"A snowflake in summer? What's happening?" she cried.

"Jack Frost's goblins must be nearby," Kirsty said worriedly.

Sunny's tiny teeth chattered with cold. "Oh, no! If they find me, they will stop me from getting back to Fairyland!"

Kirsty looked at Rachel in alarm. "Quick, we have to go!"

Rachel leaned down and lifted the fairy out of the beehive.

Sunny's golden hair dripped with honey.

"Oh, my, you're really sticky!" Rachel said.

Just then, Kirsty spotted Mrs. Merry coming out of her cottage.

"I forgot I asked for a drink," Kirsty said. "What are we going to do about Sunny?"

Rachel thought for a moment, then dropped the fairy into the pocket of her shorts.

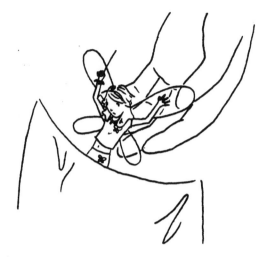

Sunny gave a cry of dismay. "Hey! It's dark in here!" she complained.

"Sorry," Rachel whispered. "I'll get you out again in a minute, I promise."

Suddenly, Kirsty noticed the open hive. "We have to put the top back on before Mrs. Merry sees it!" she said.

She bent down and grabbed the lid. Rachel helped lift it and they quickly put it into place, just as Mrs. Merry came through the trees.

"Here's your drink, dear," said Mrs. Merry, holding out a glass to Kirsty. She had taken off her strange suit, and was carrying a shopping basket in her other hand.

"Thank you very much," Kirsty said, taking the glass.

"Now, you girls stay as long as you like," said Mrs. Merry. "I must run out and buy some fish for my cat. It's time for his lunch!"

Rachel watched Mrs. Merry walk toward the garden gate. Then she slipped her hand into her pocket.

"You can come out now," she said to Sunny, gently lifting her out.

The fairy was covered with gray fuzz from Rachel's pocket. "Achoo!" Sunny sneezed and brushed angrily at the bits of sticky fuzz clinging to her wings. "I'm all clogged up!" she wailed. "I won't be able to fly."

"We can help clean you up," Rachel said. "But we'll have to be quick, in case the goblins find us."

Kirsty looked around and pointed to a stone birdbath filled with clear water. "Over there!"

"Just what we need," Rachel agreed. She carried Sunny over to the birdbath.

Sunny fluttered onto the edge of the bath, put down her wand, and dived in.

Splash!

The water fizzed and turned bright yellow. Lemony-smelling drops sprayed up into the air.

Sunny swam two circles, and before long she was sparkling clean. She zoomed up into the air to dry. Misty yellow trails appeared as she whooshed around. "That's better!" she cried.

She hovered in the air in front of Kirsty. Her wings flashed like gold in the sun. Then she swooped down onto Rachel's shoulder. "Come on, let's go to the pot at the end of the rainbow! I can't wait to see my sisters!"

Rachel nodded. She wanted to leave the garden before the goblins got there.

"Good-bye, Queenie!" Sunny called, waving to her friend. "I'll come back to visit as soon as I can!"

Queenie peeked out of the hive. She seemed a bit sad that Sunny was

leaving. Her feelers drooped as she
waved a tiny leg and buzzed good-bye.

Sunny sat cross-legged on Rachel's
shoulder as they headed for the woods.
Suddenly, she cried out and flew up into
the air. "Oh, no!" She gasped. "I left my
wand next to the birdbath!"

Rachel looked at Kirsty with concern.
"We'll have to go back," she said.

"Yes," Kirsty agreed. "We can't leave a fairy wand lying around for the goblins to find."

"Oh, dear . . . Oh, dear . . ." Sunny zipped back and forth, wringing her hands as they headed back down the path.

Rachel paused at the gate and looked into the garden. There was no sign of goblins.

Kirsty and Rachel ran through the apple trees, toward the birdbath. Sunny fluttered just above them.

Suddenly, an icy blast made them all shiver. They gazed around in alarm. Icicles now hung from the apple trees, and the whole lawn was white and crunchy with frost. The goblins had arrived! And they'd brought winter to the lovely garden.

Sunny gave a cry of horror.

An ugly, hook-nosed goblin jumped up on top of Queenie's hive. His bulging eyes gleamed. In one hand he was holding Sunny's wand!

Well Done, Queenie

"Give me back my wand!"
Sunny demanded.

"Come and get it!"
yelled the goblin rudely.
He leaped off the hive and
ran toward the gate.

Kirsty gasped as another goblin
jumped down from the apple tree.

Crunch! He landed on the frosty grass and set off at a run.

"Catch!" The goblin threw the wand to his friend. It flew through the air, shooting out yellow sparks.

The other goblin reached up and caught the wand. "Hee, hee. Got it!"

"Oh, no!" Sunny gasped.

Just then, Queenie flew out of the
hive with a loud buzz. All the other
bees swarmed behind her in a noisy
cloud.

Rachel watched, her eyes very wide.
With Queenie in the lead, the bees
formed into an arrow shape and raced
after the goblins.

"Be careful, Queenie!" pleaded Sunny.

"Get away!" The goblin shook Sunny's wand at Queenie.

More bright yellow sparks shot out of the wand. One of the sparks hit Queenie's wing. Queenie wobbled in midair. Then she buzzed angrily and flew at the goblin again.

"Help!" The goblin ducked and dropped the wand.

"Butterfingers!" grumbled the other goblin, scooping it up and continuing to run.

"They're getting away!" Kirsty cried.

Queenie and her bees rose into the air again.

"No, they're not!" Rachel cried

excitedly. The bees shot across the yard and the goblins disappeared in the angry swarm.

"Get off me!" sputtered the goblin with the wand. He tried to shoo the bees away, but tripped over his own feet. As he fell, he bumped into the other goblin.

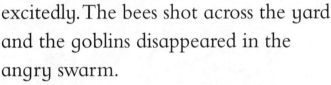

The two of them tumbled over in a
heap, dropping the wand onto the grass.

"That was your fault!" complained
one of the goblins.

"No, it wasn't!" snapped the other one.

Queenie zoomed over and picked up
the wand with one of her tiny, black feet.

She carried it straight to Sunny,
who was standing on Rachel's hand.
With a little buzz, Queenie landed next
to Sunny.

Sunny took her wand from Queenie and carefully waved it in the air. A fountain of glittering dust and fluttering butterflies sparkled around them. "My wand is all right!" Sunny cried joyfully.

"Look! The goblins are leaving," Kirsty said.

The rest of the bees had chased the goblins to the edge of the yard. Still arguing, the goblins ran across the fields.

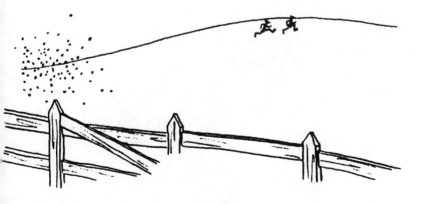

As the grumbling voices faded away, the icy wind disappeared. The sun shone warmly again and the frost melted. The bees streamed back and flew around Rachel and Kirsty, buzzing softly.

"Thank you, Queenie!" Sunny's eyes sparkled as she hugged her friend.

Suddenly, Queenie wobbled and tipped sideways.

Rachel cupped her hands, worried that Queenie would roll off. "I think she might be hurt," she said. Sunny knelt down and looked closely at Queenie. "Oh, no! She's torn her wing!" She gasped.

"It must have happened when she fought the goblin," Rachel said.

"Can you heal Queenie's wing with magic?" Kirsty asked Sunny.

Sunny shook her head. "Not on my own. But Amber or Ruby might be able to help me. We have to take Queenie to the pot at the end of the rainbow right away!"

Fairy Repairs

Rachel and Kirsty hurried across the
fields and into the woods. Rachel
carefully held Queenie in her cupped
hands, while Sunny flew behind them,
her rainbow-colored wings shimmering
in the sun.

"There's the willow tree where the
pot is hidden," Kirsty said. She went

over and parted the branches, which hung right down to the ground. The black pot lay on its side in the grass. A large, green frog hopped out from behind it.

"Bertram!" Sunny flew down and hugged him. "I'm so glad you're here!"

Bertram bowed his head. "It's a pleasure, Miss Sunny," he said. "Miss Ruby and Miss Amber will be delighted to see you."

Suddenly, a shower of red and orange fairy dust shot up out of the pot, followed by Ruby and Amber.

"Sunny!" Ruby shouted. "It really *is* you!" "It's so good to have you back!" Amber called happily. Kirsty and Rachel smiled as the fairies hugged and kissed one another.

The air around them fizzed with red
flowers, orange bubbles, and tiny,
yellow butterflies.

Ruby flew onto Kirsty's shoulder.
"Thank you, Rachel and Kirsty," she
said. "Now three of us are safe." Then
she spotted Queenie lying on Rachel's
hand. "Who is this?" she asked.

"This is my friend Queenie," Sunny
explained. "She helped me get my
wand back after the goblins stole it."

"Goblins?" Ruby shuddered.
"You were very brave to fight them,
Queenie." She flew
down and stroked
Queenie's head.

"One of the
goblins used my
wand to hurt
Queenie's wing.
Can you help her?"
Sunny asked her sisters.

Amber thought hard. "I could mend
Queenie's wing if I had a fairy needle
and thread," she said. Then she looked
sad. "But I don't have any here in
the pot."

Then Rachel remembered something. "Kirsty! What about the magic bags that the Fairy Queen gave us?"

"Oh, yes," Kirsty said. She reached into her pocket and pulled out her bag. It was glowing with a soft, silver light.

When she opened it, a cloud of glitter shot up into the air. Kirsty slipped her hand into the bag. "There's something here."

She drew out a tiny, shining needle, threaded with fine spider silk. She held it out to Amber. "Perfect!" Amber said. She flew onto Rachel's hand and sat next to Queenie.

Amber stroked Queenie's black-and-yellow head. "Don't worry," she said. "It's fairy magic, so it won't hurt."

Kirsty watched as Amber carefully wove the needle in and out of the torn wing. The row of stitches glowed like tiny silver dots.

"Look, they're starting to fade," Rachel said.

"Yes," said Amber. "When you can't see them anymore, the wing will be healed."

Queenie buzzed softly. She lifted her
head and flapped her wings. Then she
zoomed into the air. Her
wing was as good as new!
She swooped down and
landed next to
Amber. Bowing her
head, she rubbed
her feelers against
the fairy's hand.
"You have been
such a good friend
to Sunny, you
have to stay with
us," said Amber,
hugging the bee.
"Yes!" Ruby agreed. "Please
come and stay with us, just
until we go back to Fairyland."

Queenie flew over to Sunny and buzzed in her ear.

"She says she would love to," said Sunny. "There is a hiveless queen in Mrs. Merry's yard who would be happy to take care of her bees. Come on, Queenie. Let's look at our new home."

"Let's take a look, too," Kirsty said. Rachel crouched down beside her in the grass. They watched the fairy sisters and the queen bee fly into the pot.

Sunny beamed when she saw all the tiny furniture. She sat down on a soft, mossy cushion. "This is just like our home in Fairyland," she said. Then her face fell.

"But what about the rest of our sisters?
They are still trapped somewhere on the
island!"

"Don't worry," Kirsty said. "We'll
find them soon."

"Yes, we will," Rachel agreed,
jumping up. She looked at her watch.
"It's almost lunchtime. We have to go.
But we'll see you again very soon."

The fairies looked up and waved.

"Good-bye! Good-bye!" Queenie waved a tiny leg and buzzed.

Bertram, the frog footman, followed the girls out from under the willow tree. "Ruby, Amber, and Sunny will be safe here with me," he said. "But you have to be careful when you go looking for the others. Watch out for goblins!"

"We will," Rachel promised.

Kirsty looked back at the pot at the end of the rainbow. "Nothing will stop us from finding the other Rainbow Fairies!" she said.

Fern
the Green
Fairy

To the fairies at the
bottom of my garden

Special thanks to
Narinder Dhami

The Secret Garden

"Oh!" Rachel Walker gasped in delight
as she looked around her. "What a
perfect place for a picnic!"

"It's a secret garden," Kirsty Tate said,
her eyes shining.

The two girls were standing in a large
garden. It looked as if nobody else had
been there for a long, long time. Pink and

white roses grew all around the tree trunks, filling the air with their sweet smell. White marble statues stood here and there, half hidden by green ivy. And right in the middle of the garden was a crumbling stone tower.

"There was a castle here once called Moonspinner Castle," Mr. Walker said, walking up behind them. He was reading from his guidebook. "But now all that's left is the tower."

Rachel and Kirsty stared up
at the ruined tower. The yellow
stones glowed warmly in the
sunshine. They were spotted
with soft, green moss. Near the
top of the tower was a small,
square window.

"It's just like Rapunzel's
tower," Kirsty said. "I wonder if
we can get up to the top
somehow?"

"Let's go see!" Rachel
said eagerly. "I want to
explore the whole garden.
Can we, Mom?"

"Go ahead." Mrs. Walker smiled. "Your
dad and I will get the food ready." She
opened the picnic basket. "But don't be
too long, girls."

Rachel and Kirsty rushed over to the door in the side of the tower. Kirsty tugged at the heavy iron handle. But the door was locked.

Rachel was disappointed. "Oh, that's too bad," she said.

Kirsty sighed. "Yes, I was hoping Fern the Green Fairy might be here."

Rachel and Kirsty had a secret. During their vacation on Rainspell Island, they were helping to find the seven Rainbow Fairies. The fairies had been sent out of Fairyland by evil Jack Frost, and Fairyland had lost all its color without them. Fairyland would only be bright and beautiful when all seven fairies returned home again.

"Fern," Rachel called in a low voice. "Are you here?"

Here . . . Here . . . Here . . .

Her words echoed off the stones. Rachel and Kirsty held their breath and waited. But they couldn't hear anything except leaves rustling in the breeze.

"This is such a special place," Kirsty

said. "It *feels* like there's magic close by."
Then she gasped and pointed. "Rachel,
look at the ivy!"

Rachel stared. Glossy green leaves grew
thickly on the wall, but in one place the
stones were bare, in the shape of a perfect
circle.

Rachel's heart began to beat faster. "It

looks just like a fairy ring!" she said. She
had heard that when plants grew in a
circle, it was the work of fairy magic.
Rachel ran around the tower to take a
closer look and almost tripped
over one of her shoelaces.

"Careful!" Kirsty said,
grabbing Rachel's arm.

Rachel sat down on
a mossy stone to retie
her shoe. "There's
green *everywhere*," she
said, looking around
at the thick grass and
the leafy trees. "Fern
must be here."

"We'd better find her
quickly, then," Kirsty said with a shiver.

"Or else Jack Frost's goblins will find her first!"

Jack Frost had sent his goblin servants to Rainspell Island. He wanted them to stop the fairies from getting home to Fairyland. The goblins were so mean that they made everything around them turn cold and icy.

"Where should we start looking?" Rachel asked, standing up again.

Kirsty looked at her friend and

laughed. "You've got green stuff all over you!" she said.

Rachel twisted around to look. The back of her jean skirt was green and dusty. "It must be the moss," she grumbled, brushing it off.

Dust flew up into the air. It sparkled and glittered in the morning sun. As it fell to the ground, tiny green leaves appeared and the smell of freshly cut grass filled the air.

Rachel and Kirsty turned to each other. "It's fairy dust!" they cried together.

Where Is Fern?

"Fern *is* here!" said Kirsty.

"Thank goodness I sat down on that fairy dust!" Rachel said.

The girls walked all around the tower, looking under bushes and inside sweet-smelling flowers. As they walked, they softly called Fern's name. But the Green Fairy was nowhere to be found.

"You don't think the goblins have already caught her, do you?" Rachel asked. She was worried.

"I hope not," replied Kirsty. "I'm sure Fern *was* here, but now it seems like she's somewhere else."

"Yes, but where?" Rachel looked around the garden helplessly.

"Maybe there's magic around to help us," Kirsty said.

She looked down at the tiny leaves. Some of them fluttered across the garden. "I know, let's follow the fairy dust!"

The bright green leaves floated over to a
narrow path. The path led into a beautiful
orchard. Rachel could see apples, pears,
and plums growing on the trees.

"It's a magic trail!" Kirsty breathed.
"Quick, let's keep following the fairy
dust," Rachel said.
Rachel and Kirsty set off down the
path, which twisted and turned through
the fruit trees.

Suddenly, the path led them into a large clearing. Kirsty's eyes opened wide when she saw what was in front of them. "It's a maze!" she cried.

The thick, green hedges loomed above them, their leaves rustling in the breeze.

Rachel nudged Kirsty. "Look!" She pointed. "The fairy trail leads right into the maze!"

"We'll have to take that path," Kirsty said bravely.

The two girls followed the floating fairy leaves through the narrow maze entrance. Kirsty felt a little bit scared as the fairy dust led them one way, then another. What if the trail ran out and they got lost in the maze?

"Maybe there will be another clue in

the middle of the maze," Rachel said
hopefully.

"Or maybe Fern will be there!" Kirsty
added.

They turned one more corner and,
suddenly, the hedges parted to reveal the
middle of the maze.
An oak tree stood
in the very center. The
fairy dust led right to
the bottom of the tree,
then stopped.
"Fern must be
here!" Rachel said
excitedly.

Kirsty frowned.
"Yes, but *where*?" she asked, looking
around.

Tap! Tap! Tap!

The two girls jumped.

"What was that?" Rachel gasped.

There it was again. *Tap! Tap! Tap!*

Kirsty's eyes opened wide. "It's coming from over there." She pointed to the oak tree.

"I hope it isn't a trap set by the goblins," Rachel whispered.

Tap! Tap! Tap!

The noise was louder now. Slowly, Rachel and Kirsty walked around the tree. At first, they didn't see anything unusual.

Then Rachel pointed at the tree trunk. "What's a *window* doing in a *tree*?" she asked.

There was a small, hollow knot halfway up the trunk — and it was covered by a glass window!

Kirsty put out her hand and touched the window. It was very cold and wet. "It's not glass," she whispered. "It's *ice!*"

Both girls looked more closely. Suddenly, something moved behind the icy window. Kirsty could just barely see a tiny girl dressed in glittering green.

"Rachel, we've found her!" she said happily. "It's Fern the Green Fairy!"

Lost in the Maze

Fern waved to the girls through the sheet of ice. Her mouth opened and closed, but Rachel and Kirsty couldn't hear a word she was saying. The ice was too thick.

Rachel looked worried. "Fern must be freezing in there," she said. "We've got to get her out."

"We could smash the ice with a stick," said Kirsty. Then she frowned. "But Fern might get hurt."

Rachel thought hard. "We could *melt* the ice," she said.

"How?" Kirsty asked.

"Like this," Rachel replied. She reached up and pressed her hand firmly against the window of ice. Kirsty did the same. The ice felt freezing cold, but they kept pressing against it with their warm hands.

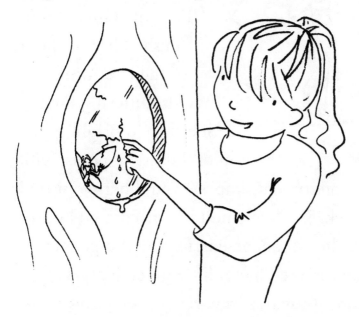

Soon, a few drops of water began to trickle down the window.

"It's melting!" Rachel said. "I think we can make a hole in it now." She gently poked the middle of the window with her finger, and the ice began to crack.

"Don't worry, Fern," said Kirsty. "You'll be out of there very soon!"

There was a sudden crack as
the ice split open. A flash
of sparkling fairy dust
shot out, leaving
behind the smell of
cut grass. And then
Fern the Green Fairy
pushed her way out
of the tree trunk, her
wings fluttering limply.
She wore a bright green
top and stretchy pants, with
pretty leaf shapes around her waist and
neck. She had small acorn-colored boots
on her tiny feet, earrings, and a pendant
that looked like a little green leaf. Her
long, brown hair was tied in pigtails,
and her thin, emerald wand was tipped
with gold.

"Oh, I'm s-s-so c-c-cold!" the fairy gasped, shivering all over. She floated down to rest on Kirsty's shoulder.

"Let me warm you up a bit," said Rachel. She scooped the fairy up and held her in her cupped hands. Then she blew gently on her.

The warmth of Rachel's breath seemed to do the trick. Fern stopped shivering, and her wings straightened out. "Thank you," she said. "I feel much better now."

"I'm Rachel and this is Kirsty," Rachel explained. "We're here to take you to the pot at the end of the rainbow." "Ruby, Amber, and Sunny are waiting for you," Kirsty added.

Fern's green eyes lit up. "They're safe?" she exclaimed. "That's wonderful!" She flew off Rachel's hand in a burst of green fairy dust and twirled happily in the air. "But what about my other sisters?"

"Don't worry, we're going to find them, too," Kirsty told her. "But how did you get stuck behind that ice window?"

"When I landed on Rainspell Island, I got tangled up in the ivy on the tower," Fern explained. "I managed to untangle myself, but then Jack Frost's goblins started chasing me. So I flew into the maze and hid in the oak tree. It was raining, and when the goblins passed by, their evil magic turned the rainwater to ice. So I was trapped."

Suddenly, Rachel shivered. "It's getting colder," she said. She glanced up at the sky. The sun had disappeared behind a cloud, and there was a sudden chill in the air.

"The goblins might be close by!" Kirsty gasped, looking scared.

Fern nodded. "Yes, we'd better get out of this garden right away," she said calmly. "You know the way, don't you?"

Rachel and Kirsty looked at each other.

"I'm not sure," Kirsty said with a frown. "Do *you* know, Rachel?"

Rachel shook her head. "No," she replied. "But we can follow the fairy trail back to the beginning of the maze."

Kirsty looked around. "Where *is* the fairy trail?" she asked.

An icy breeze was blowing all around them now. The green fairy leaves were drifting away and disappearing.

"Oh, no!" Kirsty cried. "What are we going to do now?"

Suddenly, they heard the sound of heavy footsteps coming through the maze toward them.

"I know that fairy is in here *somewhere*," grumbled a loud, gruff voice.

Fern, Rachel, and Kirsty looked at one another with wide eyes.

"Goblins!" whispered Rachel.

Fairy Fireworks

Rachel, Kirsty, and Fern listened in horror as the goblins came closer. As usual, they were arguing with each other.

"Come on!" snorted one goblin. "We can't let her get away again."

"Stop bossing me around," grumbled the other one. "I'm going as fast as I can. OW!"

Just then, there was a loud *THUD*! It sounded like someone had fallen over.

"If your feet weren't so big, you wouldn't trip over them," jeered the first goblin.

"They're big enough to give you a good kick!" the other goblin snapped.

"Let's hide in the tree," Fern whispered to Rachel and Kirsty. "I'll make you fairy-sized so we can all fit under a leaf." Quickly, she shot up into the air and sprinkled the girls with fairy dust. Rachel and Kirsty gasped as they felt themselves shrinking, down and down. It was so exciting!

Once they were small enough, Fern took the girls' hands. "Let's go," she said,

and the three of them fluttered up into
the air and landed on a branch. Fat
brown acorns grew on the tree, as big as
beach balls. Even the thinnest twigs
looked like tree trunks to the tiny girls!

Fern lifted up the edge of a leaf, which
was as big as a tablecloth, and all three
of them crept underneath.

A moment later, the goblins rushed into
the clearing.

"Where can that fairy be?" one of them
grumbled. "I know she came this way!"

They began to search around the
bottom of the tree.

"How are we going to get back to the
pot?" Rachel whispered to Fern. "Kirsty
and I aren't very good at flying. The
goblins will catch us if we try!"

Fern laughed. "Don't worry! I think I

know someone who can help us." She
pointed behind them.

Rachel and Kirsty turned to look.
A gray, furry face was peeking shyly
around the tree trunk. It was a squirrel.

"Hello," Fern called softly.

The squirrel jumped and hid behind the
trunk. Then he peeked out again, his dark
eyes curious.

"Maybe he'd like an acorn,"
Kirsty suggested.

There was a big, shiny
nut growing right next
to her. She wrapped
her arms around it,
but she couldn't pull it
off the twig. It was too
big! Rachel and Fern
came to help. All three of

them tugged at the acorn until it came
off the branch with a crack.

Fern held the acorn out to the squirrel.
"Mmm, a yummy nut!" she said.

The squirrel ran lightly along the
branch, his long, furry tail waving.
He took the acorn and held it in his
front paws.

"What's your name?" asked Fern kindly.

"I'm Fluffy," squeaked the squirrel, between nibbles.

"I'm Fern," said the fairy. "And these are my friends Rachel and Kirsty. We need to get away from the goblins. Will you help us?"

Fluffy shivered. "I don't like goblins," he squeaked.

"We won't let them hurt you," Fern promised, stroking his head. "Can you give us a ride on your back? You can jump from hedge to hedge much better than we can! We have to get out of this maze."

"Yes, I'll help you,"

Fluffy agreed, finishing the last piece of
his acorn.

Rachel, Kirsty, and Fern climbed
onto the squirrel's back. Kirsty thought
it felt like sinking into a big, soft
blanket.

"This is great," said Fern, snuggling
down into the squirrel's fur. "Let's go,
Fluffy!"

The squirrel turned and ran along the
branch. Rachel, Kirsty, and Fern clung
tightly to Fluffy's thick fur as he jumped

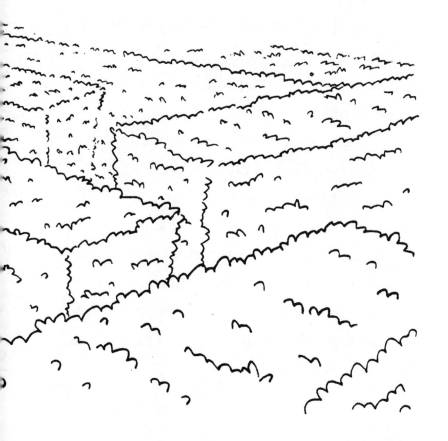

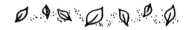

out of the tree, right over the goblins' heads! He landed on the closest hedge. The goblins were so busy arguing, they didn't even notice.

Fern leaned forward to whisper in the squirrel's ear. "Well done, Fluffy. Now, the next one!"

Rachel gulped when she saw how far away the next hedge was. "Maybe Fluffy needs some fairy magic to help him," she said.

"No, he doesn't," Fern replied, her green eyes twinkling. "He'll be fine!"

Fluffy leaped into midair. He sailed across the gap and landed safely on top of the next hedge. Rachel and Kirsty grinned at each other. This was so exciting! It was a bit bumpy, but Fluffy's fur was like a soft cushion. The squirrel

was moving so fast, it wasn't long before they had left the goblins far behind.

"We made it!" Fern said at last, as Fluffy reached the edge of the maze. "Now, which way do we go, girls?"

Rachel and Kirsty looked at each other in dismay. "This isn't how we came *in*,"

Rachel said. "I don't know the way
back to the pot from here. Do you,
Kirsty?"

Kirsty shook her head.

Fern looked worried. "But I have to get
back to the pot!" she said. "That's where
my sisters are!"

"Oh!" Kirsty had an idea. "Rachel,
what about looking in our magic bags
for help?"

"Good idea," Rachel agreed.

Titania, the Fairy Queen, had given Rachel and Kirsty two special magic bags, for whenever they needed help rescuing the fairies. The girls took the bags with them everywhere, just in case.

Kirsty opened her backpack and looked inside. One of the magic bags was glowing with a silvery light. "I wonder what's inside," she said, reaching in.

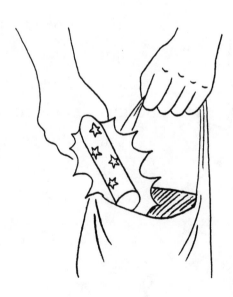

She pulled out a thin, green stick
covered with sparkling gold stars.

"It looks like a *sparkler*," Rachel said.
"That's not much use, is it?"

"It's a fairy sparkler!" said Fern
excitedly. "I can use it to write a message
in the sky, and my sisters will see it from
the pot. Then they'll know we need help."

"But what about the goblins?" Rachel
asked. "Won't they see it, too, and know
where we are?"

Fern looked serious.
"We've got to take the risk,"
she said. Fern held the
sparkler in one hand, her
wings fluttering. She
lit the top with her
wand and quickly flew
up into the sky.

Rachel and Kirsty held their breath.
Fern and the sparkler shot upward,
trailing bright green sparks behind them.
Fern flew higher and higher into the sky,
and used the sparkler to write a message
in a shower of emerald stars. The stars
spelled out the words:

They twinkled brightly in the darkening sky before fading away.

"We won't have to wait long," Fern said, landing beside Rachel and Kirsty on the ground. "Help will come very soon."

Rachel and Kirsty wondered what would happen. How could the fairies come to their rescue? They weren't

supposed to leave the pot at the end of the rainbow, in case the goblins found them. Suddenly, the leaves behind Rachel, Kirsty, and Fern rustled.

"Did you see the fairy sparkler?" shouted a loud goblin voice. "It came from over there. Quick, before that fairy gets away again!"

Hedgehog Help

Rachel and Kirsty looked at each other in alarm. Fluffy seemed scared, too. The goblins were on their trail again!

"They're coming toward us," Rachel whispered as the goblin voices got louder.

"Don't worry," Fern said, smiling. She didn't seem nervous. "My sisters will send help quickly."

Just then, Rachel spotted a line of
golden sparkles twinkling toward them
through the fruit trees. "What's that?" she
whispered.

"Is it goblin magic?" Kirsty asked,
suspicious.

Fern shook her head. "They're
fireflies! My sisters must have sent them
to show us the way back to the pot."

Suddenly, there was another shout from
inside the maze. "Look, what are those
lights over there?"

"The goblins have spotted the fireflies!" Rachel gasped.

"Quickly, Fluffy!" Fern said as they all climbed onto the squirrel's back again. "Follow the fireflies!"

The golden specks were dancing away through the trees. Fluffy scampered after them, just as the goblins dashed out of the maze.

"There's the fairy!" one of them shouted, pointing at Fern. "Stop that squirrel!"

"Come back!" the other roared as Fluffy ran off.

Rachel, Kirsty, and Fern
clung to Fluffy's fur as the
squirrel zigzagged back
and forth to get away
from the goblins.
Fluffy scrambled
up the trunk of the
nearest tree. He was
just about to jump across
to the next, when someone
called to them from below.
"Hello!"

"Who's that?" Rachel asked. She,
Kirsty, and Fern peered
down at the ground.
A hedgehog was
standing at the foot of
the apple tree. "Hello!"
he hollered again.

"The animals in the garden have heard that you're in trouble. We'd like to help."

"Oh, thank you!" Fern called. Then she gasped as the two goblins appeared among the trees.

"Where'd that squirrel go?" one of them yelled.

Quickly, Fluffy leaped across to the next apple tree. The goblins roared with anger and dashed forward. At that moment, the hedgehog curled himself into a ball and rolled right into their path. Rachel thought he looked like a big, prickly soccer ball.

"OW!" both goblins howled. "My toes!"

Rachel and Kirsty couldn't help laughing as the goblins jumped around holding their feet. "Hooray for Hedgehog!" the girls shouted.

As Fluffy jumped from one fruit tree to

the next, the firefly lights behind them
began to go out.

"Hey! Who turned off the lights?"
wailed one of the goblins, still rubbing
his foot. "Which way are we supposed
to go?"

"How should I know?" snapped the
other goblin. Their voices were getting
fainter now as Fluffy hurried on.

"Thank you, fireflies!" called Fern,
waving at the last few
specs of light. "We
need to find our
way to the orchard
wall from here. We
can't be far from
the pot now."

"If I were
human-sized, I

could probably figure out which way to go," Kirsty said. "But everything looks so big and unfamiliar!"

"But if we go back to our normal sizes, the goblins will surely spot us!" said Rachel.

"I can help you," a small voice whispered. A fawn was standing at the bottom of the tree. Her golden brown coat was short and silky, and she stared up at them with big, brown eyes.

"You mean you can show us the way?" Kirsty said.

"Yes, I can." The deer nodded, twitching her little tail. "I can show you a shortcut."

She trotted off through the trees on her long legs. Fluffy followed her, leaping from branch to branch above the little deer's head.

Rachel was so excited she could hardly breathe. She was riding on a squirrel's back, being shown the way to the pot at the end of the rainbow by a fawn!

A few moments later, they reached the brick wall that ran around the outside of the orchard. Fluffy leaped up to the top of the wall, and Rachel and Kirsty looked eagerly ahead of them. On the other side of the wall was a meadow, and beyond that was a patch of woods.

"Look!" Rachel shouted. "That's where the pot is!"

Flying High

"Thank you!" Kirsty and Rachel called to the baby deer. She blinked her long eyelashes at them and trotted away.

A blackbird with shiny, dark feathers was sitting on the wall nearby. He hopped over to them. "I'm here to take you to the pot at the end of the rainbow," he chirped. "All aboard!"

267

Fluffy looked sad as Fern, Rachel, and Kirsty slid off his back and climbed onto the blackbird. It was a tight squeeze, and the bird's feathers felt smooth and silky after Fluffy's thick fur.

"Good-bye, Fluffy!" called Rachel. She blew him a kiss. "And thank you!" She felt sad to leave their new

friend behind. Then the blackbird soared
into the air.

"Look for the big weeping willow tree,"
Rachel told the blackbird as he swooped
over the meadow.

"I can't wait to see my sisters again,"
said Fern, sounding very excited.

The blackbird flew over the woods and

landed in the clearing near the willow
tree. Rachel, Kirsty, and Fern jumped
down onto the grass, calling good-bye to
the blackbird.

"Who's there?" croaked a
stern voice. A plump,
green frog hopped
out from under
the hanging branches
of the tree.

"Bertram, it's me!" Fern
called. Quickly, the fairy
waved her wand, and Rachel and
Kirsty shot up to their normal size again.

"Miss Fern!" Bertram said joyfully.
"You're back!"

"We followed the fireflies," Fern said,
giving the frog a hug. "Thank you for
sending them."

"We saw the sparkler in the sky,"
Bertram explained, "so we knew you
were in trouble. But you'll be safe here,"
he went on. "The pot is hidden under
the tree. The goblins have no idea that
it's here!"

Rachel and Kirsty hurried over and
pulled aside the long branches. The pot at
the end of the rainbow lay there on its side.

Suddenly, a fountain of red, orange, and
yellow fairy dust whooshed out of the
pot. Ruby, Amber, and Sunny flew out,

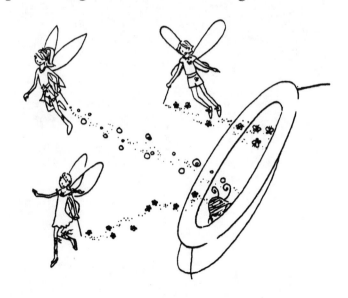

looking very excited. A big queen bee
buzzed out behind them.

"Fern!" Ruby called. "You're safe! It's so
good to see you!"

Rachel and Kirsty beamed as they
watched the fairies hug one another. The
air around them fizzed and popped with

red flowers, orange bubbles, yellow butterflies, and green leaves.

"We really missed you," said Sunny. The bee nudged her with a tiny feeler. "Oh, sorry, Queenie," said Sunny. "This is my sister Fern."

Queenie buzzed, "Hello!"

"How did you get back so quickly?" asked Amber. "We sent the fireflies only a little while ago."

"Our forest friends helped us," Fern said. She waved as the blackbird flew off. "Especially Fluffy the squirrel." She sighed. "It was sad to leave him behind."

Ruby laughed. "Who's that, then?" she asked, pointing at a tree on the other side of the clearing.

Rachel and Kirsty looked, too. Fluffy was peeking at them from behind the tree trunk, looking very shy.

"Fluffy!" Fern flew over and hugged him. "What are you doing here?"

"I was worried about you," Fluffy explained shyly. "I wanted to make sure you got back to the pot safely."

"Would you like to stay with us, too?" asked Amber. "You could live in the willow tree, couldn't you?"

"Yes, *please*," squeaked Fluffy. "I'm very

lonely. I live in that oak tree inside the maze all by myself!"

Ruby turned to Rachel and Kirsty. "Thank you again," she said. "I don't know what we'd do without you!"

Fern fluttered lightly onto Rachel's shoulder. One of her wings brushed softly against Rachel's cheek, like a butterfly. "We'll see you again soon, won't we?"

"Yes, of course," Rachel promised.

"Only three more Rainbow Fairies left to find!" Kirsty added. She took Rachel's hand and they waved to the fairies, then ran out of the clearing. "We'd better get back to your mom and dad, Rachel. They'll be wondering where we are."

"Good idea." Rachel laughed. "If we don't hurry back, my dad will eat the whole picnic by himself!"

Ruby, Amber, Sunny, and Fern are safe.
Now Rachel and Kirsty must look for

Sky the Blue Fairy!

But where could she be? Follow along
with Rachel and Kirsty in this special
sneak peek. . . .

A Magic Messenger

"The water's really warm!" Rachel
Walker laughed. She was sitting on a
rock, swishing her toes in one of
Rainspell Island's deep blue tide pools.
Her friend Kirsty Tate was looking for
shells nearby.

"Be careful not to slip, Kirsty!" called

☆ ✿ ☆ ☆ ☆ ✿ ☆

Mrs. Tate. She was sitting farther down
the beach with Mrs. Walker.

"OK, Mom!" Kirsty yelled back. As she
looked down at her bare feet, a patch of
green seaweed began to move. There was
something blue and shiny underneath it.
"Rachel! Come here," she shouted.

Rachel went over to Kirsty. "What is
it?" she asked.

Kirsty pointed to the seaweed.

"There's something blue under there,"
she said. "I wonder, could it be . . ."

"Sky the Blue Fairy?" Rachel said
eagerly.

Jack Frost had banished the seven
Rainbow Fairies from Fairyland with a
magic spell. Now they were hidden all
over Rainspell Island. Until they were
all found, there would be no color in

Fairyland. Rachel and Kirsty had
promised the Fairy King and Queen to
help find them.

The seaweed twitched.

Rachel felt her heart beat faster.

Read the rest of

Sky the Blue Fairy

to find out what magic
is hiding in the shiny seaweed.

A fairy for every day!

The seven Rainbow Fairies are missing! Help rescue the fairies and bring the sparkle back to Fairyland.

When mean Jack Frost steals the Weather Fairies' magical feathers, the weather turns wacky. It's up to the Weather Fairies to fix it!

Jack Frost is causing trouble in Fairyland again! This time he's stolen the seven crown jewels. Without them, the magic in Fairyland is fading fast!

■ SCHOLASTIC
www.scholastic.com

FAIRY